P9-AQE-589

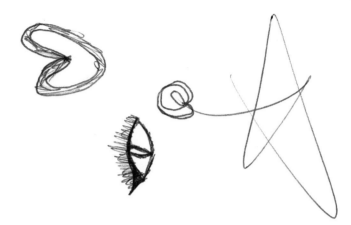

Walruses

Walruses

Charles Rotter

THE CHILD'S WORLD®, INC.

Published in the United States of America by The Child's World®, Inc.
PO Box 326
Chanhassen, MN 55317-0326
800-599-READ
www.childsworld.com

Product Manager Mary Berendes
Editor Katherine Stevenson
Designer Mary Berendes
Contributor Bob Temple

Photo Credits
ANIMALS ANIMALS © Richard Kolar: 30
© Carleton Ray, The National Audubon Society Collection/Photo Researchers: 15
© 2000 Dominique Braud/Dembinsky Photo Assoc. Inc.: 2
© Erwin & Peggy Bauer: 9, 23
© Francis Caldwell/Visuals Unlimited: 20
© 1990 Harry M. Walker: 6
© Henry H. Holdsworth: 29
© Ingrid Visser/Ursus Photography: 13
© Paul Nicklen/Ursus Photography: 19, 24, 26
© Phil A. Dotson, The National Audubon Society Collection/Photo Researchers: 16
© 1996 Rod Planck/Dembinsky Photo Assoc. Inc.: cover, 10

Library of Congress Cataloging-in-Publication Data
Rotter, Charles.
Walruses / by Charles Rotter.
p. cm.
Includes index.
ISBN 1-56766-894-1 (library bound : alk. paper)
1. Walrus—Juvenile literature. [1. Walrus.]   I. Title.
QL737.P62 R68 2001
599.79'9—dc21
00-010777

On the cover...

Front cover: This large male is resting on an Alaska beach.
Page 2: These walruses are sleeping close together in the sunshine.

Table of Contents

It is a sunny day in the far north. Ocean waves crash and splash against the rocky shore. On the rocks, hundreds of huge animals are stretched out, napping in the sunshine. They have small heads, fat bodies, and short flippers instead of legs. One of the animals waddles and slithers to the edge of the water, then dives right in. What is this strange creature? It's a walrus!

What Are Walruses?

Walruses are **mammals,** which means that they have warm bodies and feed their babies milk from their bodies. They are also **pinnipeds**—sea mammals that have flippers instead of arms and legs. Seals and sea lions are pinnipeds, too.

Walruses can grow very large—some males can weigh more than 3,500 pounds! They have thick, wrinkled, brownish skin and square heads with small, round eyes. Walruses also have long teeth called **tusks.** A walrus's tusks, just like an elephant's, are made of **ivory.** But a walrus's tusks are much shorter—only up to about three feet long.

This large male walrus is resting on some ⇒
rocks near Round Island, Alaska.

A walrus uses its tusks in many different ways. It uses them as weapons when it fights. It might use them to dig up food from the sea bottom. A walrus even uses its tusks to pull itself out of the water, called "hauling out."

Although an adult walrus has almost no hair on its body, it does have hairs on its face. These hairs, called *vibrissae* (vy–BRIH–see), make a walrus look as though it has a mustache. A walrus's vibrissae are very sensitive to touch, just like a cat's whiskers. The walrus uses its vibrissae to find its way through dark water. It also uses them to find food.

⇐ Here an adult is "hauling out." You can see its tusks digging into the dirt as it pulls itself ashore.

Where Do Walruses Live?

Like their close relatives—seals and sea lions—walruses spend a lot of time in the ocean. They live along the coastlines of the Arctic, far to the north. The Arctic is so cold that the ocean is often covered with ice. But walruses don't seem to mind the cold. They often come out of the water and sit on top of floating chunks of ice.

This walrus is resting in the snow on a sunny afternoon. ⇒

Most walruses live in different places at different times of the year. They tend to follow the edge of the sea ice. In the summer, the ice in the southern Arctic melts. The walruses head north, where temperatures are cooler and there is still ice on the sea. They often ride on chunks of ice drifting in the water. When fall comes, the temperature drops and ice builds up again farther south. The walruses then head south. This movement from place to place is called **migration.**

This walrus is on the edge of the ice in the Chukchi Sea. ⇒

How Do Walruses Stay Warm?

Living on ice and in the half-frozen seas, walruses must have a way to stay warm. They have almost no hair to act as a blanket. Instead, they have a thick layer of fat, called **blubber,** under their skin. The blubber holds in the walrus's body heat, protecting the animal from the icy cold. Other sea mammals, such as seals and whales, have a layer of blubber, too.

⇐ This bull's blubber keeps it warm as it swims off Alaska's coast. It's skin has turned white from the cold water. When the walrus rests in the warm sunshine, its skin will turn pink again.

What Do Walruses Eat?

Walruses eat many different kinds of food. They like to snack on clams, starfish, and other animals that live in the sea-bottom mud. They also eat octopuses and fish. A hungry walrus will even use its great tusks to attack seals.

This adult is diving for food in the cold Arctic. ⇒

Walruses gather in large groups called **herds.** At certain times of the year, thousands of walruses live together. One place known for its walrus herds is Round Island, off the coast of Alaska. Thousands of walruses gather there every year. Some older walruses on Round Island don't travel with the seasons anymore. They stay there year round, lounging in the sun.

Walruses communicate with each other by touching and smelling. Adults often shelter their babies with their flippers or fall asleep using other walruses as pillows! The main way walruses communicate is by making sounds. Adults often grunt, snort, growl, or even bark to let other walruses know how they feel.

⇐ The walruses in this large herd are sleeping together on a Round Island beach.

The herd's male walruses are called **bulls.** Bulls are able to make an underwater sound that females can't—a sound like a ringing bell. When a bull makes this sound, some scientists say the walrus is "pinging." The pinging walrus might be warning his neighbors to stay away. He might also be trying to attract female walruses, called **cows.**

This two-year-old walrus is swimming underwater. ⇒

A walrus cow normally has one baby at a time. The young walrus, called a **calf,** is helpless without its mother. The cow takes care of her calf for a long time. She protects it and feeds it milk from her body. By the time the calf is about two years old, it can take care of itself and find its own food.

Walruses don't have many enemies, but the ones they do have can be very dangerous. Both killer whales and polar bears eat walruses. Killer whales sometimes catch full-grown walruses swimming in the water. The walrus might try to defend itself with its tusks, but a killer whale is bigger, stronger, and faster. Polar bears can catch only small walruses that are out of the water. They often catch calves resting on the shore.

⇐ This walrus calf is staying safe by resting on its mother's back. A polar bear is less likely to attack a calf when the mother walrus is nearby.

27

Some people also hunt and kill walruses. Native people in some parts of the Arctic survive by hunting walruses. They use every part of the animals they kill. They eat the meat and use the skins to make boats. They make tools from the walrus's tusks and bones.

This long-tusked male lives in a protected ⇒ area near Round Island, Alaska.

Sadly, countless walruses have been killed just for their tusks. The tusks' ivory was sold and carved into jewelry and other objects. Like elephants, walruses were overhunted to the point where their future was in danger.

Fortunately, laws were passed to protect walruses in many areas. Though some hunters still kill walruses illegally, the number of walruses has grown steadily. Walruses are safe for now. As long as we're careful, these fascinating creatures will continue to swim and dive in the cold Arctic waters.

⇐ This walrus lives in a New York aquarium.

Glossary

blubber (BLUB-ber)
Blubber is a thick fat layer under the skin of walruses, whales, and other ocean mammals. The blubber keeps the animals warm.

bulls (BULLZ)
Bulls are male walruses. Walrus bulls sometimes fight with their tusks.

calf (KAFF)
A baby walrus is called a calf. The calf stays with its mother for about two years.

cows (KOWZ)
Cows are female walruses. A walrus cow usually has only one baby at a time.

herds (HERDZ)
Herds are groups of animals that live together. Walrus herds sometimes number in the thousands.

ivory (EYE-vree)
Ivory is the hard white substance that makes up walrus and elephant tusks. Many walruses have been killed for their ivory.

mammals (MAM-mullz)
Mammals are animals that have hair or fur and feed their babies milk from their bodies. Walruses are mammals.

migration (my-GRAY-shun)
Migration is a movement from one place to another during the year. Walruses migrate from south to north and back again, following the melting and freezing sea ice.

pinnipeds (PIN-nih-pedz)
Pinnipeds are mammals that live in the sea and have flippers instead of legs or arms. Walruses are pinnipeds, and so are seals and sea lions.

tusks (TUSKS)
Tusks are large teeth that grow out of an animal's mouth. A male walrus's tusks can grow to about three feet long.

Web Sites

www.seaworld.org/walrus/walrus.html

www.pbs.org/wnet/nature/toothwalkers/index.html

Index